NÚMERO UNO

by **Alex Dorros** and **Arthur Dorros**

illustrated by **Susan Guevara**

ABRAMS BOOKS FOR YOUNG READERS
NEW YORK

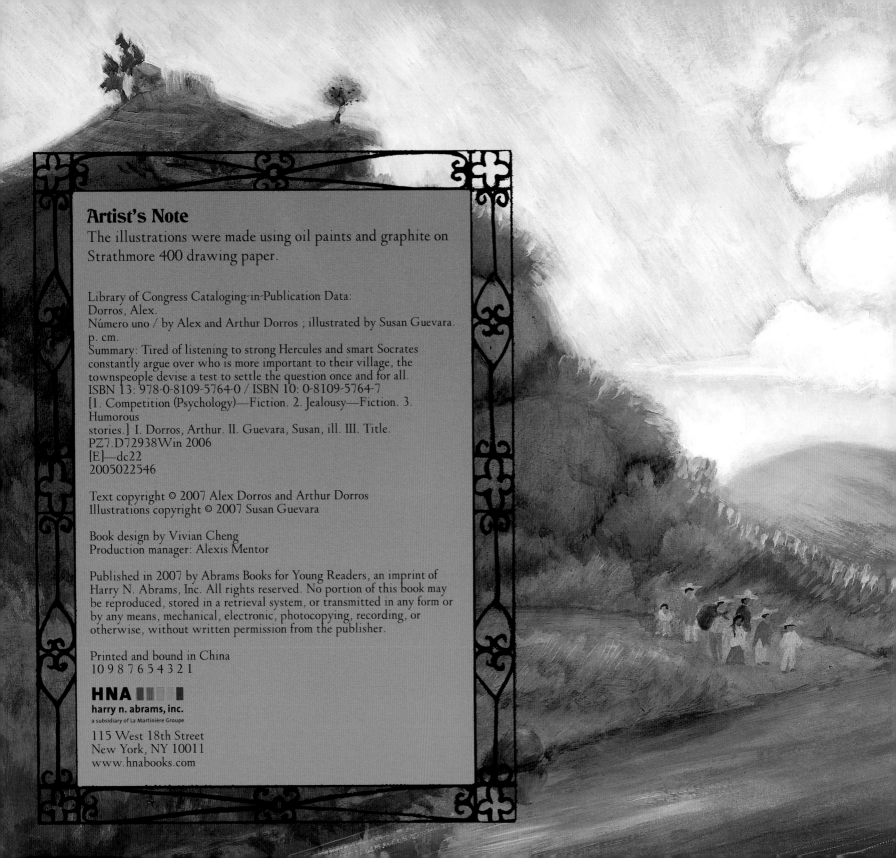

Artist's Note

The illustrations were made using oil paints and graphite on Strathmore 400 drawing paper.

Library of Congress Cataloging-in-Publication Data:
Dorros, Alex.
Número uno / by Alex and Arthur Dorros ; illustrated by Susan Guevara.
p. cm.
Summary: Tired of listening to strong Hercules and smart Socrates constantly argue over who is more important to their village, the townspeople devise a test to settle the question once and for all.
ISBN 13: 978-0-8109-5764-0 / ISBN 10: 0-8109-5764-7
[1. Competition (Psychology)—Fiction. 2. Jealousy—Fiction. 3. Humorous
stories.] I. Dorros, Arthur. II. Guevara, Susan, ill. III. Title.
PZ7.D72938Win 2006
[E]—dc22
2005022546

Book design by Vivian Cheng
Production manager: Alexis Mentor

Printed and bound in China
10 9 8 7 6 5 4 3 2 1

HNA
harry n. abrams, inc.
a subsidiary of La Martinière Groupe

115 West 18th Street
New York, NY 10011
www.hnabooks.com

Para la mejor, Sandra Marulanda
–Alex D.

For Susan Van Metre and Jason Wells, both *número uno*
–Arthur D.

For Christophe and Trav
–Susan G.

Hercules and Socrates lived in a village in the mountains.
Each said he was more important to the village.

Hercules said it was because he was strong.
"*Soy fuerte.*"

Socrates said it was because he was smart.
"*Soy inteligente.*"

They were always arguing.

When the villagers wanted to know how to make a bridge across the river, they called Socrates. He thought and figured and planned. Socrates said that because of his ideas, he was the most important. "*¡Número uno!*"

"*¡No!*" Hercules said.

"*¡Sí!*" said Socrates.

When the villagers wanted help building the bridge, they called Hercules. He lifted and carried and climbed. Hercules said that because of his strength, he was the most important. "*¡Número uno!*"

"*¡No!*" said Socrates.

"*¡Sí!*" said Hercules, kicking over a pile of stones to demonstrate.

Socrates hid the plans for the bridge, so no one was sure what to do.

¡Basta!

The two men argued and argued.
"¡Basta!" Enough, an old man told them.
"Tengo una idea." A young boy said he had an idea for how to settle the argument once and for all. Hercules and Socrates would leave the village for three days. While they were gone, the villagers would keep working on the bridge and see who was missed most. Socrates and Hercules each hoped it would be himself.
"¡Yo!" Me, Socrates said.
"¡Yo!" Me, said Hercules.
"¡Basta!" said the old man.

The two agreed to go to the mountain near the young boy's house to wait.

Hercules said he would get to the top of the mountain first.

Socrates insisted he would arrive first.

They raced to the top of the mountain, each in his own way.

When they reached the mountaintop, they were hungry.
Socrates figured out where to find food. He told Hercules
that this proved ideas and thinking were most important.

"¡No!" said Hercules.

"¡Sí!" said Socrates.

They argued until they fell asleep.

The second night, it was cold. Hercules gathered wood and slammed two rocks together to make a fire to keep them warm. He said to Socrates that this proved strength was more important.

"¡No!" said Socrates.

"¡Sí!" said Hercules.

They argued most of the night.

The third day, they anxiously peered toward the
village, trying to see how the bridge building was going.
A storm rumbled in. Lightning crackled, thunder
pounded, and rain pelted them both.

To get out of the storm, they found a cave. A boulder blocked the entrance. Hercules pushed and pushed on it. The boulder did not budge. Socrates brought a branch and wedged it under the rock. The boulder still did not budge.

They tried to argue about how to move
the boulder, but they could not hear each
other. So they moved closer together.

Hercules pushed on the boulder, while
Socrates stood on the branch.

The boulder rolled out of the way.

"¡Inteligencia!" Intelligence, said Socrates.

"¡Fuerza!" Strength, said Hercules.

They argued all night.

The next morning, they stumbled tiredly back to the village to find out who was most important.

"¿Yo?" Hercules asked if it was him.

The villagers said that without Hercules' strength, the work had been very difficult. Hercules was happy; strength was most important!

"¿Yo?" asked Socrates.

The villagers said that without Socrates' ideas, it had been difficult to figure out what to do. Socrates was thrilled. His intelligence was most important.

"¡Yo!" Me, he said.

"¡No, yo!" No, me, said Hercules.

"*¡Basta!*" Enough, the old man said.
The villagers had missed both Hercules and Socrates. Some strength
was important, some intelligence as well. The winner, said the young
boy who had thought of the contest, was the village.

What they had not missed, he said,
was Hercules and Socrates arguing.

"*¿Yo?*" Who, me? asked Hercules.
"*¿Yo?*" Me? asked Socrates.